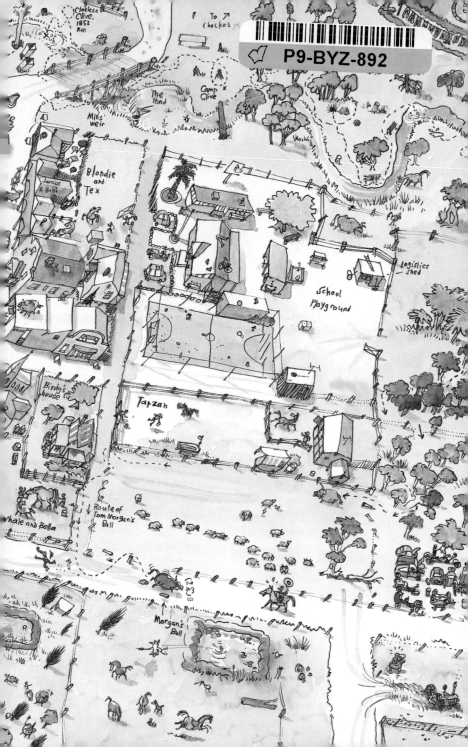

For Holly —A. L.
For Oppy —R. H.

First published in the United States in 2009 by Chronicle Books LLC.

Text © 2008 by Alison Lester.
Illustrations © 2008 by Roland Harvey.
Originally published in Australia in 2008 by Allen & Unwin under the title *Racing the Tide*.

North American type design by Molly Baker.
Typeset in Berkeley.
Manufactured in China.

Library of Congress Cataloging-in-Publication Data
Lester, Alison.
[Racing the tide]
The sea rescue / by Alison Lester ; illustrated by Roland Harvey.
p. cm. — (Horse crazy ; bk. 3)
Summary: During summer vacation in rural Australia, best friends Bonnie and Sam are taking care of two horses and helping with sheep shearing when they stumble upon a crime at Skull Rock.
ISBN 978-0-8118-6940-9
[1. Horses—Fiction. 2. Abalones—Fiction. 3. Poaching—Fiction. 4. Australia—Fiction.] I. Harvey, Roland, ill. II. Title. III. Series.
PZ7.L56284Se 2009
[Fic]—dc22
2008052605

10 9 8 7 6 5 4 3 2 1

Chronicle Books LLC
680 Second Street, San Francisco, California 94107

www.chroniclekids.com

HORSE crazy

THE SEA RESCUE · 3

by Alison Lester

illustrated by Roland Harvey

chronicle books · san francisco

Christmas Is Over

Christmas had come and gone, and again neither
Bonnie nor Sam got the horse they wanted from
Santa. Sam and her dad, Bill, spent Christmas
Day in the city with her cousins. Bonnie's
parents, Chester and Woo, hosted a huge family
lunch at Peppermint Plain. Now all that was left
was the decorations.

Sam stared up at the beautiful Christmas tree in Bonnie's living room. Woo was an artist and she always made crazy Christmas trees. This year she had filled an old tank with dead eucalyptus branches, sprayed them silver and gold, and hung red paper cranes from them.

"I made three and Chester made one, but Mom made all the rest," Bonnie said proudly.

Vacation!

Now that Sam was back from the city, vacation could really begin. It was a delicious feeling having all of January just for fun, and to make it even better, the girls had horses to ride too.

Sam's father was the local policeman and he always let the girls ride his mare, Drover, when he didn't need her for police work. The girls shared a secret about Drover and loved double-dinking on her, but having a horse each was even better.

Janice and Bob, who ran the newsstand, were going away for a week's vacation and had asked Bonnie and Sam to take care of their horses. The girls had spent the last weeks of school planning their horsey vacation. Of all the horses in Currawong Creek, Blondie and Tex were two of their favorites. Blondie was a beautiful palomino quarter horse, who could sometimes be moody.

Tex was an appaloosa with a pink nose. He had the sweetest nature a horse could have. Nothing shocked Tex.

"Who do you want to ride?" Sam asked, looking at the map of Wild Dog Hills.

"I don't mind." Bonnie traced Currawong Creek with her finger. "Let's see how it works out. Where will we go first?"

"I'm sorry to spoil your plans, girls." Woo looked embarrassed. "I forgot to tell you, Bonnie. Violet and Woody asked if you'd help them with sheep shearing next week and I said you would. I didn't know you and Sam had plans."

"How could you, Mom?" Bonnie rolled her eyes. "We always have plans!"

If she and Sam didn't have Blondie and Tex for the week, Bonnie would have loved the thought of helping out Aunty Vi and Uncle Woody. Their farm, Banksia Ridge, was right on the coast, and the bush and beach were full of surprises.

Bonnie's dad, Chester, had two older sisters: Aunty Birdy, who knew everything about horses, and Aunty Violet, who knew everything about sheep. They both thought Bonnie was the best thing since sliced bread.

"Maybe Sam can go with you. You two would have a fabulous time," said Woo.

"We've promised Janice and Bob, though," said Bonnie. "Can't we go and help them *after* we look after Blondie and Tex? That way we can do both things."

"No." Woo shook her head. "They have to shear next week. The shearing team is booked in. They go to the same farms at the same time every year."

"Why do they have to do it now?" Bon was like a dog with a bone when she argued. "Why organize it for the middle of vacation?"

"It actually makes sense, Bonnie. The lambs have all been sold, so they don't have to put them through the yards. And it's getting hot. It's the perfect time for the ewes to have their woolly coats removed. There's nothing more to say. I promised them you'd help and that's what you're going to do."

Making Plans

"We've got two days to ride before you have to go." Sam was trying to cheer Bonnie up as they waited for Janice at the newsstand. Bonnie was flipping through a copy of *Horse Deals*. She loved looking at all the beautiful horses for sale.

"Look at this pinto that's been stolen." Bonnie opened the page for Sam to see. "He looks like a black and white version of Bella."

"Hi girls!" Janice came from the back of the shop with a stack of newspapers. "How are my horse-sitters this morning?" Janice was dressed like a cowgirl, as usual, with sequinned horse shoes on her shirt and a big silver belt-buckle.

"It's not good, Janice. Bon has to go and help her aunt and uncle with the shearing the day after tomorrow. I'll still be able to look after Blondie and Tex, but we were really looking forward to riding up in the mountains together."

"Where's their farm?" Janice turned to get another pile of papers. She was always on the move. If you wanted to talk to her you had to go with her.

"Out on the coast," Bonnie called after her. "Out at Whale Bay."

Bonnie and Sam pushed past the photocopier and the card rack to the kitchen at the back of the shop.

"Whale Bay is only about twenty miles away," Janice said over a cup of tea. "You could ride out." Bonnie and Sam stared in stunned silence at Janice's good idea.

"You should both go and help with shearing and take Blondie and Tex with you. They'd love it, though Tex doesn't like getting his feet wet. He hates water." She turned to go. "Maybe you can persuade him to go for a swim."

The farrier came the next day to put new shoes on Blondie and Tex for the ride out to Banksia Ridge. The girls loved Clint and he never minded their questions. "See how I'm bending the tip of the nail a little bit?" Half under Tex, Clint held up the hammer and nail so the girls could see. "A little bend like this makes sure the nail angles out, not in, where it would hurt. The nails are beveled anyway, but I like to do an extra bit, just to be sure."

The paddock behind Janice and Bob's newsstand was like an oven. Blondie dozed as she waited for her turn and Tex was half asleep too. Clint's little

dog, Cactus, and Sam's dog, Smartie Pants, hung
around Clint as closely as the girls. The dogs
made happy growling sounds as they chewed on
hoof clippings.

Clint gently put Tex's hoof down and stood
up and stretched his back. "Whale Bay, huh?"
He took his tools across to Blondie and reached
down for her hoof. "They reckon there's some
serious abalone poaching going on out there."

Poachers!

"What are abalone?" Sam had never heard the word.

"They're those big shells, Sam." Bonnie patted Blondie's neck as Clint began to trim her hoof. "You know those mother-of-pearl shells that people use as bowls and in jewelry? They have a disgusting slimy thing that lives in them. It's like a sucker, clings to the rocks. You have to dive down and pry them off with a screwdriver."

"Why would anyone poach them?"

"They're worth a fortune. Some people think they're delicious. They are really yummy, once they're cleaned and cooked. If you have a license you can take five a day, I think. There's a limit, to protect them, so they don't become extinct. Woo dives for them sometimes at the Cape but I've never wanted to. You have to go down through the kelp, and there are big black stingrays there."

Clint threw a curve of trimmed hoof and Cactus and Pants chased after it. "Abalone is big business," he said. "A commercial license to get them is worth more than a million dollars and the abalone meat sells for nearly fifty dollars a pound. There'll always be a black market for it." Sam passed him a shoe. "Your dad will be able to tell you more about it, but word at the pub is that Soggy Stevens is at it again. He's been caught heaps of times, had his boat confiscated and everything, but he's done his time and now he's got another boat. He takes the boat down to Whale Bay every day and dives—says he's doing research . . . as if. The police know he's diving for abs but they can't catch him with any in the boat. It's a mystery."

That evening Sam asked her father about Soggy Stevens.

"Soggy's been to jail and fined more times than I can remember and he still won't stop. He's addicted to diving for abalone," Bill said, shaking his head. "I'd love to catch him at it."

Sam pushed her baked beans around the plate. Sometimes when Bill was busy with police work his dinners weren't very exciting.

"Well, maybe Bon and I will find some evidence while we're at Whale Bay."

After dinner Sam walked around to visit
Bonnie's Aunt Birdy. She had promised to lend
the girls her saddlebags for their long ride.

"This would be a good place to stop for lunch,"
Aunt Birdy said, finger on the map. "Platypus
Creek. You'll be able to give the horses a drink
and I think there's even a picnic table there."

Bonnie would bring the food and drinks
when she came into town tomorrow for their
early start, but Sam still found plenty to prepare:
sunscreen, insect repellent, and candy. She
packed her bag, too, for the week. It felt good to
be on the brink of an adventure.

Setting Out

"Good luck! Look out for cars!" Aunt Birdy had helped the girls saddle up, and now she waved them on their way.

"I'll see you there when I bring your bags out!" Bill called.

Sam rode Blondie, and Bonnie rode Tex. They felt like cowgirls riding through the main street of Currawong Creek. It was so early the stores were still closed.

"It's like in a movie, when the baddies ride into town and everybody goes inside," joked Bonnie.

"Yeah," said Sam. "*Yee haw!* Let's go!" The horses broke into an eager canter and, with Pants at their heels, clattered up the deserted street and out onto the coast road.

It was a still, sunny day and the old dirt road to the coast was quiet. If a car did come the girls would hear it from a long way away and get onto the shoulder. They rode through open farmland where white-faced cattle stared at them in silence and magpies perched in lines on gates, warbling as they passed.

Sometimes the road
wound through the bush
and dappled shade made
the morning air cool.
A kookaburra swooped past them,
and on one straight stretch a lyrebird scurried
across the road, his lacy tail trailing behind.

It took all morning to get to Platypus Creek.

"This must be it, Sam." Bonnie looked down
at a small grassy flat, where a creek gurgled
around one side and tall eucalyptus trees made
patches of shade. They rode the horses down the
gentle bank to water them at the creek. Blondie
waded right in, so the water was just below her
belly, but Tex stayed at the edge. No matter how
sweetly Bonnie whispered to him in horse talk
or how persistently she nudged him with her
heels, the spotty horse would not budge.

"I don't think we'll be going swimming at
Whale Bay," Sam said.

Woo had made corned beef sandwiches for
lunch. Bonnie whistled to Pants so she could

feed her the crusts, but Pants took a long time to come to the picnic table.

"What's she got in her mouth?" Sam put her sandwich down. "Come here." Pants presented her find. "Pee-ew! It stinks!" She took a closer look. "Hey, Bonnie, it's one of those shells!" It was an abalone shell, with some abalone meat still inside it.

"That was dumped only a couple of days ago, Sam." Bonnie had her detective face on. "And what's it doing here, so far from the sea?"

"Show us, Pants," Sam urged the little dog. "Show us where you got it."

They followed her along the creek a short way, and there, behind a patch of tea-tree, was a big pile of silver shells.

"It's got to be poachers, Sam." Bonnie's eyes were huge. "There must be a hundred shells here."

Banksia Ridge

The girls saw the sea for the first time as they
rode up from Platypus Creek, then spent all
afternoon getting closer to it. When they crested
the last big hill they could see paddocks stretched
out behind Whale Bay and the house and sheds,
sheltered by the ridge of banksias that gave the
farm its name. The road was a sand track now
and the horses' hooves were soft upon it.

Six sheepdogs raced out barking as the girls approached the sheds, bearing down on Pants like a gang of bullies and sniffing her all over.

A piercing whistle sent them all flying back and a skinny figure appeared, wiping his hands on his trousers.

"That's Uncle Woody," Bonnie told Sam.

The old man turned to the house as he walked toward them. "Vi!" he bellowed. "Our drovers are here!"

Sam had never seen such a messy farm. Bonnie's father, Chester, believed in putting things away, and Peppermint Plain was as tidy as a park. Here at Banksia Ridge, there was stuff everywhere: old trucks and cars, tractors, rusty farm machines, sheds, pens, and almost hidden by a wild garden, the house, with a sagging red roof.

Vi showed them where to tie the horses while they unsaddled and washed them down. The enormous, leaning shed was full of dusty harnesses and saddlery, cracked and perished with age.

Vi noticed Sam staring. "Yes, we used to have a lot of horses out here. My father, Bonnie's grandfather, sowed all this country to pasture using horses. In the olden days, this place and Peppermint Plain were part of the same cattle run."

Pants barked suddenly, her "I-hear-Bill's-car" bark, and sure enough, his police car pulled up at the shed.

As Bill carried their bags to the house, Sam told him about the abalone shells at Platypus Creek, and he congratulated the girls on their fine detective work.

"There's something strange going on, that's for sure," sniffed Uncle Woody. "We've seen some lights at night, down the beach and out at sea."

"That's right," said Aunty Vi. "Down toward Skull Rock."

Drover Girls

The next day Bonnie and Sam worked all morning mustering sheep and droving them back to the shearing shed. Aunty Vi rode a quad bike and Uncle Woody followed behind in the battered pickup. "Since my hip seized up it's the only way I can get around," he explained to Sam.

The collie dogs skulked around the sheep like spies, cutting off escapees and barking at the slowpokes. The youngest dog, Barney, kept doing the wrong thing until Vi got sick of yelling and made him sit behind her on the bike.

Bonnie was used to herding cattle and sheep, but Sam had never been a drover before. It took a while to figure out how to make the sheep go the way you wanted them to, but once they took off, the mob flowed across the paddock like lava.

By lunchtime, three hundred sheep were locked in the pens under the shearing shed, ready to be shorn the next day.

"Now it doesn't matter if it rains," said Vi.

"You can't shear them if they're wet," Bonnie explained to Sam.

The Hut

After lunch Bonnie and Sam followed the track across the sand dunes to go riding on the beach. Indigo clouds hung over the horizon, leaking columns of rain into the sea. The horses snorted and propped when they saw the wide expanse of the beach and crashing surf. At the water's edge Blondie plunged straight in, splashing through the shallows like a toddler.

"Come on, boy," Bonnie whispered to Tex. "It's only water. You'll love it."

But Tex would not go in. He ducked and danced and scurried sideways like a crab to avoid even the tiniest creeping line of foam.

When the girls swapped horses, he was just as stubborn for Sam, ignoring her drumming heels like he'd ignored Bonnie's horse talk. So they gave up and cantered down the beach, letting the horses race for a little way, then

easing them back to a canter, a trot, and finally
a walk.

"That's Skull Rock." Bonnie pointed. "We have
to watch the tide here. If it comes in too far we
won't be able to get back."

"And look!" Sam was pointing inland. "There's
a hut."

They rode up to a small wooden building nestled in the shelter of the dunes. It was weathered silver-grey and a lopsided tank held rainwater from the roof. The only door opened on to a veranda. Through the small windows the girls could see two beds and a table.

"Wouldn't it be great to come and stay here," they said at the same time.

"Of course you can go and stay there." Aunt Vi seemed just as excited as Bonnie and Sam. "You'll have a lovely time at the old shepherds' hut. Our kids used to go down there when they were young."

After dinner they walked out to the beach, Woody leading the way with his flashlight, to look for phosphorescence.

"We call them glow bugs," Bonnie told Sam. "Sometimes we see heaps of them. They slosh in on the waves then fade on the sand."

Tonight there were no glow bugs, just the moon shining on the dark sea, and a starry sky. When they turned to go home, Sam spotted a dancing light on the sea. "What's that?" she called out, but it disappeared as soon as she spoke. Suddenly it flickered again.

"That's down at Skull Rock," said Vi. "It's that same light we've been seeing for months now."

"Maybe it's abalone smugglers," said Sam.

"Maybe it is," said Vi in a spooky voice. "Or maybe it's the ghost of Skull Rock."

Shearing

"You're going to be busier than a dog with two tails," Woody told the girls at breakfast. And he was right. By 7:30, the two shearers, Max and Jimmy, had started shearing—tipping the big ewes onto their bottoms and holding them with their legs. They trimmed all the matted or dirty wool off with the first blow of their shears, then stroke by stroke cut off the creamy fleece.

Jimmy's grandson was the rouseabout, picking up the dirty scraps and bagging them, sweeping the floor, and flinging the fleeces onto the slatted table for the wool inspector.

Bonnie and Sam brought the sheep up from under the shed to the holding pens and made sure the catching pens were full. The shorn sheep looked naked and skinny without their thick fleece, and it was funny to see them sliding down the chutes to the outside pens.

Bonnie and Sam kept tally of how many sheep each shearer shore in a dog-eared book.

Smartie Pants loved being a sheep dog, barking and diving in now and then to nip. In the shed all the collies wore muzzles so they couldn't bite, but they barked like banshees. If they had to get somewhere in a hurry they ran across the sheeps' backs like tightrope walkers.

When they stopped for tea on the first morning, Sam was exhausted. But that was only the beginning. She and Bonnie did all sorts of jobs. They helped pile the wool into the bale press, gave Woody a hand with the cooking, pushed the sheep into the pens, passed Vi the drenching gun and marking paint, and finally drove the shorn sheep back to their paddocks.

At the end of the second day they sat on the steps of the grand old shed and waved good bye to the shearers.

"Well done, girls." Vi put her arms around Bonnie and Sam. "You've been a wonderful help. We couldn't have done it without you."

That night, all four of them fell asleep at the dinner table.

Overnight Adventure

Bonnie and Sam slept in until late the next morning. In the kitchen, Vi had put everything they needed for their stay at the shepherds' hut into extra saddlebags.

"I won't tell you what food I've packed," she said. "That way it'll be a surprise for you. The old stove works well but make sure there are no birds' nests in the chimney before you light it." She held up a mobile phone. "And I'm putting this in too. Just in case you need to call us."

They had a big shearer's breakfast of eggs and bacon, added sleeping bags and clothes to the bags, then saddled the horses and set off. The rain clouds had passed and it was a beautiful summer's day with hardly a breath of wind.

When they got to the hut they checked that the bush paddock was safe and secure for the horses, then they settled in. Sam found an old

broom and swept the floor. Bonnie turned the
mattresses over to make sure there was nothing
creepy underneath, then laid their sleeping bags
out. Their food fit on the shelves above the table
and there were driftwood pegs to hang their
clothes on. They collected wood for the stove
and put their flashlights on the table, ready
for dark. Then they flopped on the beds and
enjoyed the feeling of having their own house.

"I feel like a swim," said Bonnie.

Sam jumped up. "Good idea. Let's take the horses bareback and try again with Tex."

The sea was like a big turquoise pond and there were no waves in the bay between the hut and Skull Rock. Blondie walked straight into the deep water until she was swimming. Sam held her mane and floated beside her, then lay on her back again as they came back to shore.

"Have a go on Blondie," she called to Bonnie. "She loves it."

Tex still wouldn't go in the water. They stood the horses side by side and crawled across to swap. "It's a mid-air horse transfer," Sam said.

Bonnie cantered Blondie back into the sea then practiced her trick-riding skills, standing on Blondie's back, then diving off with a somersault.

Sam tried various ways to get Tex into the water: bossing him, tricking him, and begging him. Pants even started barking at him, but nothing worked.

"You are an old stupid Tex," she said, exasperated. "If you tried it, you'd love it."

Vi's surprise dinner was sausages that Bonnie and Sam cooked on the old stove, then rolled up in white bread with tomato sauce.

"Mom and Dad would freak out if they knew we had a fire," said Bonnie.

"Yes. I think Vi is used to big kids," said Sam. She peeped in the firebox. "We'll just make sure it's out before we go to bed."

Afterward, they made hot chocolate with powdered milk and dipped their cookies in it. They brushed their teeth and spat off the edge of the veranda then climbed into their sleeping bags. By flashlight Sam read aloud a story from an old school reader that Vi had put in the saddlebag. It was about a girl and boy who swam their horses out to rescue some people from a shipwreck, more than one hundred years ago. Before Sam finished, both Pants and Bonnie were snoring, so she turned off the flashlight and fell asleep too.

Ghosts!

Bonnie sat up, her heart pounding. Something had woken her.

Pants was sitting up on Sam's bed, hackles up, growling.

"Sam!" Something thumped the outside of the hut. "Sam!" Bonnie shook her sleeping friend. "Wake up, Sam! There's something outside."

When the girls peered out the back window they screamed together. There *was* something there!

Pants barked sharply.

"What is it, Sam?" Bonnie's teeth were chattering. "It looks like two ghosts."

Sam peeped out the window again, then leaned forward, staring. She started to laugh.

"What is it, Sam? Why are you laughing?" Bonnie grabbed at Sam's legs.

"It's Blondie and Tex," said Sam. "I guess

they're sheltering from the wind. They *do* look like ghosts."

When Bonnie looked into the dark she laughed too. The horses were standing, heads down, with their rumps toward the hut.

"They look like ghosts with no heads." Bon was relieved to have been frightened by something so harmless. "Maybe they're the headless horsemen of Shepherds' Hut."

The sound of the sea that had seemed sinister when she was afraid now soothed her. The two girls and their dog drifted into sleep.

In the morning Bonnie woke up with a feeling that she had forgotten something. Something kept niggling at her mind. They had breakfast in bed: bananas, granola, raisins, and milk in plastic bowls. As she sat there, staring at the door, it suddenly came to her. She thought hard, in case it was just her imagination, but now she could definitely remember.

"Somebody opened the door last night."

"What?" Sam choked on her granola.

"That's what woke me. I can remember now. The door opened and a flashlight shone in the hut."

"Are you sure you weren't dreaming, Bon?" Sam asked her friend.

"No, I heard footsteps going off the veranda too. Maybe I couldn't remember last night because it would have been too scary."

"You *must* have been dreaming," Sam insisted.

Pants whined politely at the door and Bonnie got up to let her out. "Ooohh!" She gasped, looking out, then reached down to the floor for something and showed it to Sam. "This isn't a dream," she said. "This is a flashlight and a rope."

The shepherds' hut suddenly felt a long way from anywhere and she was glad they had Vi's mobile. Sam dialed her home number and waited anxiously while the phone rang.

"Hi, Dad. It's me, Sam," she said, surprised that tears welled in her eyes at the sound of his voice.

When she explained what had happened, Bill said they should pack up and ride back to Banksia Ridge.

"Just to be on the safe side," he said. "There's probably a rational explanation, and whoever it was will be long gone, but I'd feel better if I knew you were out of there. I'll ring Woody and Vi and let them know you'll be back for lunch. Maybe when I come to pick up your bags tomorrow we'll have a look around."

They rolled up their sleeping bags and swept the floor again.

"The good thing about a tiny house like this is that there's hardly any housework," said Bonnie, taking one last look.

"Yep," said Sam. "It's a lovely hut. I wish the night visitor hadn't spoiled it for us." She twisted the latch on the door, making sure it was shut properly. "Let's go and catch the horses."

More Evidence

Bonnie and Sam walked through the bush at the back of the paddock, calling for the horses. The sky was cloudy again and tiny finches flitted through the trees. When they found the horses they used a stump to get on.

"Don't you love riding bareback?" asked Bonnie.

"Yes," Sam agreed. "Especially when the horses have their smooth summer coats."

They rode toward the hut, following the fence. The horses suddenly propped, staring.

"What's that?" Sam peered through the trees.

"It's a car. A four-wheel drive with a boat trailer," Bonnie whispered.

The horses stood quietly while the girls looked at the car. Nothing moved.

"Let's go a bit closer," said Bonnie. "But be ready to skedaddle if there's anybody there."

They rode right up to the fence and peered over it. "There's nobody here." Sam felt uneasy. "They must be out in the boat, I guess. But why would they be here?"

"It must be the abalone poachers, Sam," said Bonnie. "Try to remember the license plate number and we'll phone your dad."

"I'll scratch it on my reins with a stick," Sam said, breaking off a small branch. Bonnie read out the number for her, then they kicked the horses into a canter and rode back to the hut.

While Bonnie saddled the horses, Sam called her father again.

"That's Soggy's car," said Bill when Sam told him the number. "I'm leaving Currawong Creek now. I know the track that leads out to Skull Rock and I'll drive out there to make sure I don't miss them." His voice rose. "But I want you and Bonnie AWAY from there! Do you hear me, Sam? Don't mess around, just get going."

The girls were ready in record time, scared now. "I'm taking these, too," Bonnie shoved the flashlight and rope into a saddle bag. "It's evidence."

They trotted away from the hut, and it felt good coming onto the wide expanse of the beach, where nobody could sneak up on them.

The sea was different today, rough and noisy.

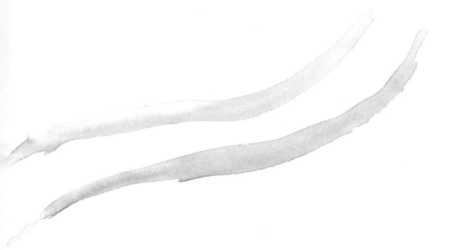

They saw the tire marks immediately. They couldn't miss them: a big curve where the car had turned around, then straight into the sea where the boat had been unloaded. Bonnie followed the tracks until Tex danced away from the waves.

"More evidence, Sam," she yelled above the waves.

Sam looked out to sea, searching for a boat. She couldn't spot it, even though she peered like a hawk. The surf was boiling, and farther out the waves glittered and danced.

"Maybe they're behind Skull Rock!" she yelled
to Bonnie. She shifted her focus to the rock and
thought she saw something. "Look, Bonnie!" She
pointed. "Their boat must have sunk!" Three
tiny figures were clinging to the base of Skull
Rock. "I can hear them calling for help."

"I thought that was birds," said Bonnie. "But
it's screaming."

Sam could see why the men were screaming. Skull Rock was as smooth as a skull, and the base where they were standing was already underwater.

The tide was coming in and soon there would be nothing for the men to hold on to.

As the girls watched, a huge wave sloshed against the rock and knocked the figures down.

"They're going to drown, Bonnie," said Sam.

So many thoughts raced through Sam's mind that it felt like a big railway station. She dug into her saddlebag for the cell phone and called Bill's number. She yelled into the phone, telling him the situation, but she couldn't hear what he said over the pounding waves.

"Tell Woody and Vi to come!" she screamed.

"They're not going to get here in time, Sam." Bonnie stared out to sea. "Look! That wave went right over them!"

"Follow me." Sam trotted Blondie above the high tide mark. She unbuckled the saddlebags and dropped them on the sand. "No point getting all this stuff wet," she said. "Can you pass me that rope they left on the veranda, please?"

"You're not, Sam!" Bonnie's eyes were as big as an owl's. "You can't swim Blondie out and save them. That was just a story."

"We have to, Bon. We can't just leave them drowning. They all have moms and dads, maybe kids. They might even have kids at our school."

She tied the green rope to the horn of her saddle. "Anyway, Blondie will do it easy. And we can be heroes."

Blondie went straight into the surf. The big waves didn't faze her at all. She swam right through them.

Pants raced up and down in the shallows, barking. Bonnie watched her friend clinging to the palomino as the waves broke over them.

"Please, Tex," she begged. "Please go in." She booted him hard. "Sam needs us."

Tears of frustration blurred her vision as the stubborn appaloosa balked at the shallows. But then he moved forward into the water.

"I love you, Tex!" Bonnie shouted as they crashed through the waves after Blondie.

Heroes

Blondie felt like a big, safe ship. All Sam had to do was to hang on tight. They were on the less windy side of Skull Rock, where the waves weren't so big.

"Can you swim this far?" Sam yelled to the men.

The one with the mustache gave a thumbs up. That must be Soggy, thought Sam. They pushed away from the rock on a big swell and swam toward her, two men supporting the third, who was limp and bleeding from the head. Sam felt suddenly afraid. They looked like drowned rats but they were much bigger and stronger than her. She threw the rope toward them.

"Don't come any closer!" she shouted, but they kept coming. Suddenly Blondie lunged at the swimmers, baring her big yellow teeth. With her mane wet and her ears back she looked like a dragon. "She'll bite your face off!" Sam shouted. "Hang on to the rope!" She turned Blondie toward

the shore and saw Bonnie and Tex just clearing
the last breaker. Tex held his chin up high.
You could see that he hated getting wet. "You
champion, Bon!" Sam shouted, her fear ebbing.
Bonnie took the end of the rope and they towed
the drowning men to shore between them.

"Look, Sam!" Bonnie pointed. "There's your
dad!" The police car was racing along the beach.
Sam dropped the rope and cantered to meet it.

"Are you all right?" Bill shouted. "Are you both
all right?"

Sam nodded. She suddenly felt teary again.
A helicopter came thudding over the sand
dunes and suddenly the beach was crowded.
Vi and Woody's pickup came screaming down
the beach, the collies all barking in the back.

Bonnie and Sam rode the horses up to the sand dunes, away from the action. Blondie drew the line at helicopters. She snorted and danced as Sam slid off her. The girls leaned against each other and Pants wriggled between them.

"I'm shaking," said Bonnie.

"Me too." Sam showed her wobbling hand. "But we saved them, Bon."

Abalone Explanations

The helicopter finally lifted away, taking the injured man to the hospital. The other two sat with blankets around them, drinking cups of tea and telling Bill their story. For months Soggy had moored his catch of abalone to a buoy near Skull Rock then returned at night to pick them up. Last night a huge wave had swamped the

boat. "We always use the shepherds' hut to store dry clothes and gear. Young Lofty got a hell of a fright last night when he found you girls there," Soggy said. "But it was a good thing. We would've been history if it wasn't for you and your horses."

Bonnie and Sam cantered behind Vi and Woody's pickup, following them back to Banksia Ridge. Pants ran with the collies, swerving at seagulls. Blondie shifted into the shallows and Tex moved with her, sending spray flying as they raced along.

Home Again

Bonnie and Sam let the horses pick at the long grass beside the road and looked down at their town. Currawong Creek was just the same.

There were no TV cameras waiting for them. Bill made sure their rescue didn't turn into a circus, and let them give just one interview to the *Currawong Creek Chronicle*.

"Janice will be pleased that we got Tex to have a swim," said Bonnie. "Let's go and tell her."